In My Own Shoes

The Adventures of

From bookshelf to yours! I hope you enjoy this adventure! Charmane Echols

Charmane Echols

Illustrated by
Laurie H. Brady

SEASON
Press LLC

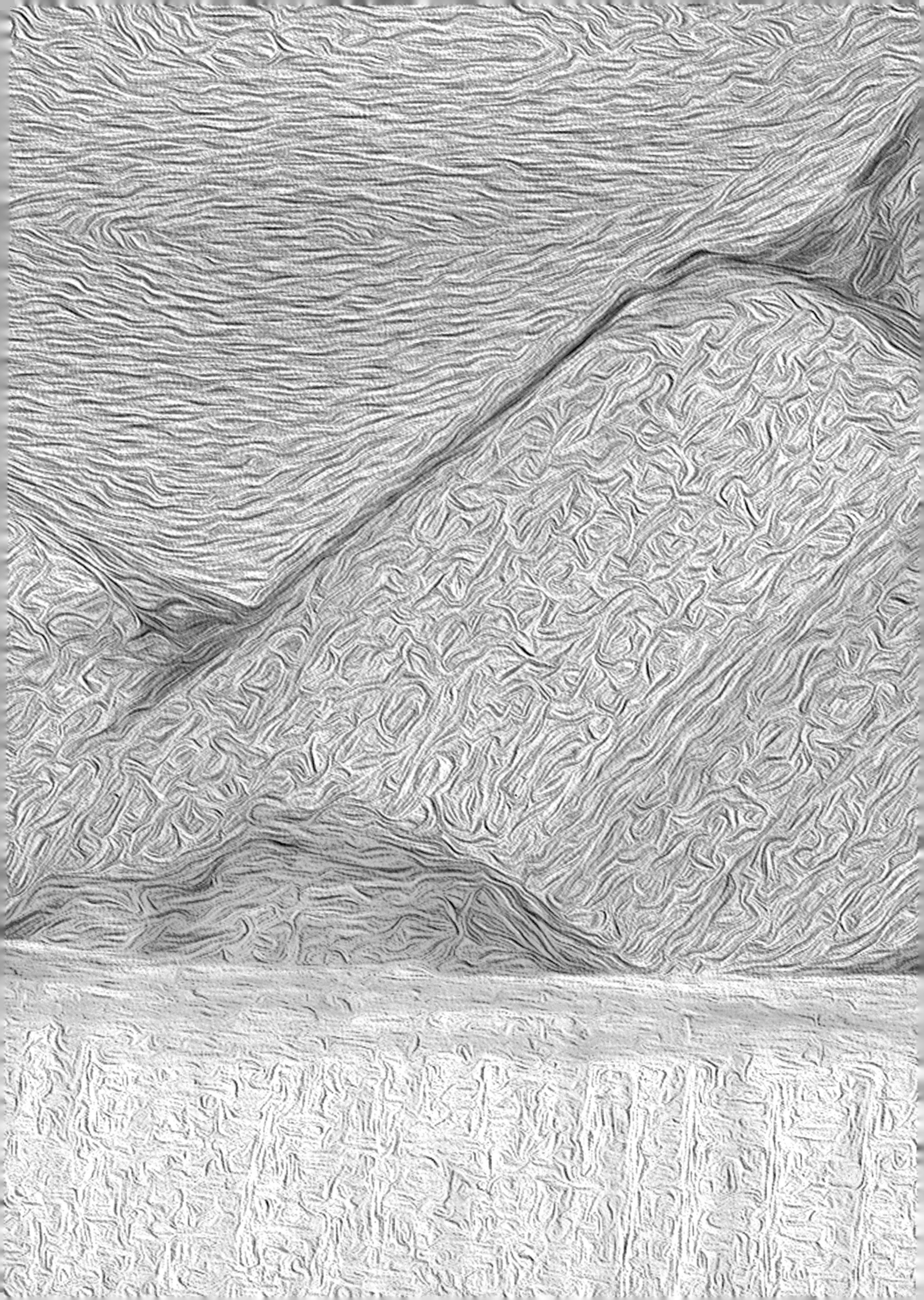

Kimberlite took her favorite apron off the hook, wrapped the strings around her waist, and tied it into a clumsy bow. She loved to help her mother prepare the bread dough for dinner. They mixed the dough. They kneaded the dough. They molded the dough. Then, they placed it into the large black oven to bake. As the bread began to bake, Kimberlite became very hungry.

The bread seemed to be taking forever to bake, so Kimberlite went out to relax on their small wooden porch. She missed her siblings, who were away at school.

"One day, I'll get up in the morning, get a lunch pail, and go to school too!" Kimberlite pouted to the baby squirrel that busied himself looking for nuts.

Kimberlite smiled, as she smelled the beautiful rhododendrons that were in full bloom. She reached into her pocket, and pulled out the nugget of coal her father gave her for her 5th birthday. He worked in the coalmines of Virginia just like his daddy, and granddaddy.

When his last baby girl
was born, he decided to name
her, Kimberlite, because it meant,
diamond.

Daddy promised to one day, find his
daughter a rare diamond that shined
so much brighter than a lump of coal.
Each day, she dreamed of the
beautiful diamond her mother
said could be found on
the side of the
mountain hidden
among the
coal.

As soon as
she heard her
daddy whistling up
the road, she ran to him.

"Daddy, Daddy, did you find it? Did you find a diamond that shines so much brighter than a lump of coal?"

"Not today, Baby. Not today. But you know, I will never stop looking for it, right?"

"I know Daddy," she said as he picked her up, hugged her, and kissed her on the forehead.

Kimberlite thought, "It's taking too long for him to find that diamond. I'm just going to have to find it myself."

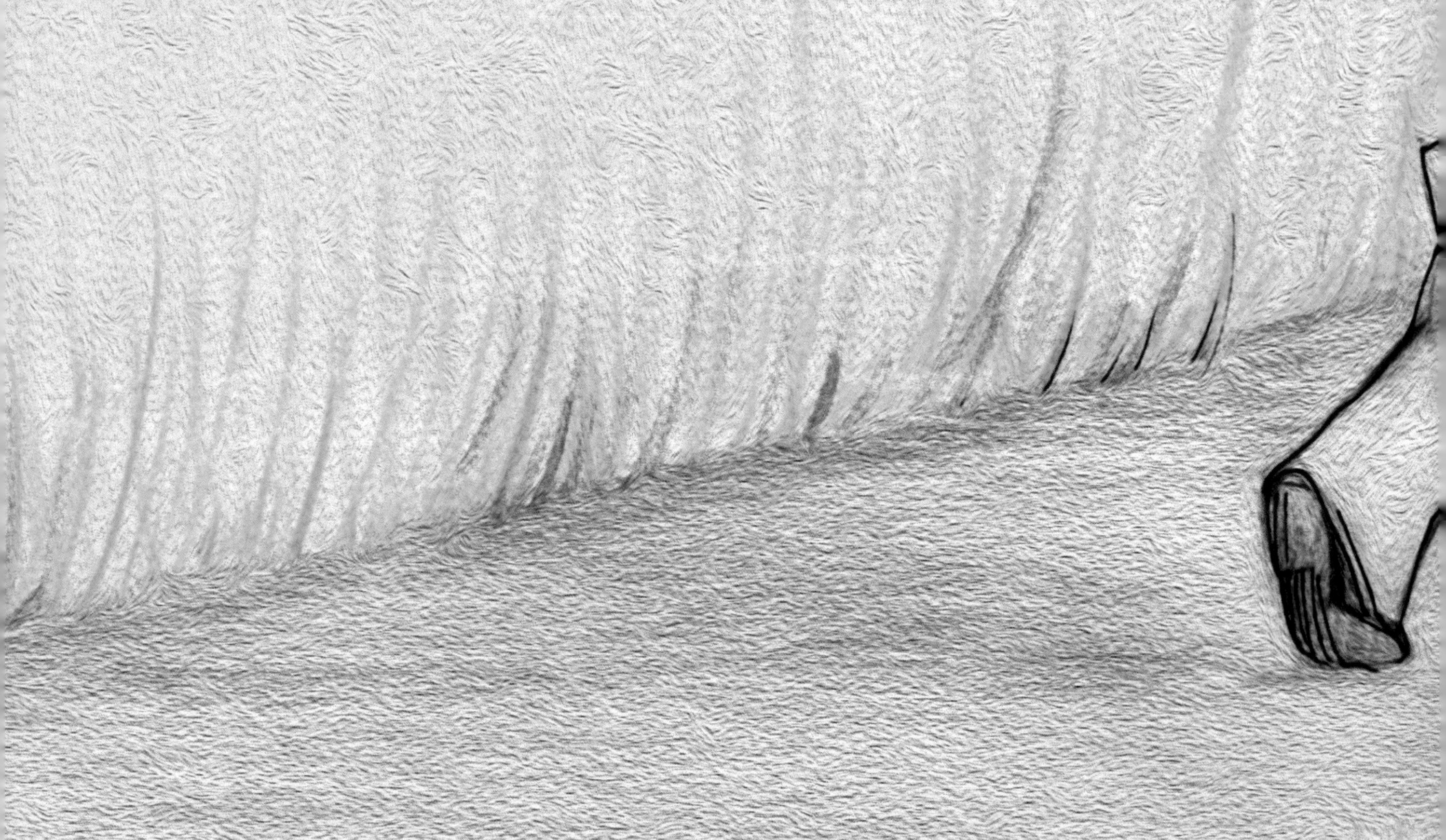

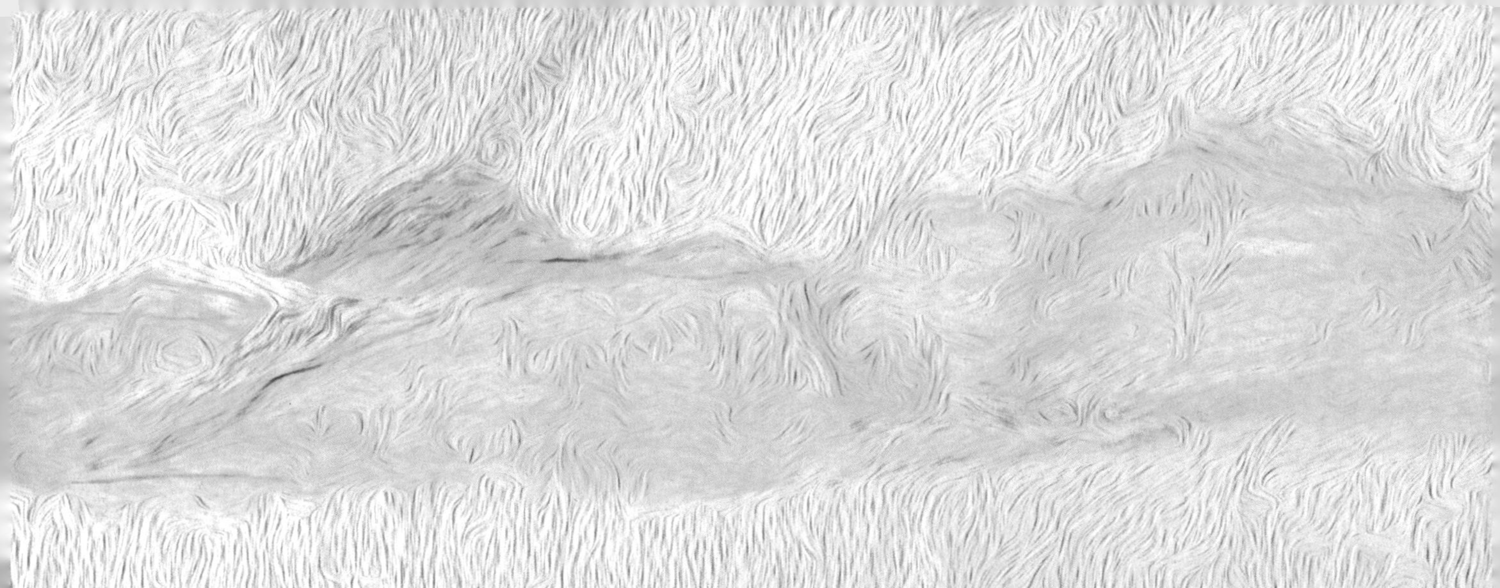

The next morning, after her brothers went to school, and Daddy headed off to the mine, Kimberlite made her move. She thought of ways to get the diamond that shined so much brighter than a lump of coal. The only way, was through the hollow. The hollow was a long, dark trail in a small valley between the hills of the mountain. It was a cold, dark, and lonely place.

“I am not afraid,” Kimberlite said to herself.

She grabbed her backpack, and placed in it a pair of her father’s work shoes, and her nugget of coal. His shoes were five times bigger than hers, but she knew they would come in handy.

Kimberlite skipped along the meadow. Before she knew it, her home was far behind her. She passed the road, and headed along a trail. She reached a long, dark, winding path that her brothers had talked about. It was the path that led to the hollow.

She heard sounds from animals she had never heard. She felt eyes starring at her that she could not see. But, she knew she could make it through.

Suddenly, she heard a rattling voice hiss, "I can see you. I know you are looking for the diamond that shines so much brighter than a lump of coal. But, is not real."

Kimberlite was afraid of the talking rattlesnake, but she puffed her chest, and stood her ground.

"I know the beautiful diamond that shines brighter than a lump of coal IS real!"
When the rattlesnake saw that Kimberlite was not going to back off from her hunt, he agreed to help her. "Well, well," he hissed. "Follow me."

Kimberlite and Rattlesnake
continued through the hollow.

Suddenly, a cougar roared,
"What are you doing over here?"

Kimberlite and Rattlesnake jumped. Kimberlite wanted to run, but Rattlesnake eased toward Cougar, and bowed before him.

"Oh, hello Mr. Cougar," Rattlesnake hissed. "I'm showing this young girl the way to the other side of the mountain."

Cougar roared in anger. Rattlesnake and Kimberlite trembled in fear.

"Rattlesnake, you KNOW that is not the right way!" Cougar said, as he leaped toward Rattlesnake, and almost stepped on his head.

"Little girl, run along the railroad tracks that way, now!" Cougar roared to Kimberlite.

"As for you Rattlesnake, I'll take care of you."

Kimberlite ran with all her might, and never looked back. After it seemed she had been running forever, Kimberlite slowed down to catch her breath. She realized the trail had become so dark that she could not see ahead. She heard the blast of a train whistle in the distance, and crackle of thunder. Rain began to fall, and Kimberlite ran for cover under a Sycamore tree near the creek.

She had been traveling for such a long time. If she were home, this would be her naptime. She yawned, sat down under the tree, and placed her backpack on the ground to use as a pillow. Before she knew it, she fell asleep.

As the storm ended, Kimberlite awoke, refreshed. She looked out and saw the top of the mountain ahead of her.

"Almost there!" she said as she gathered her backpack.

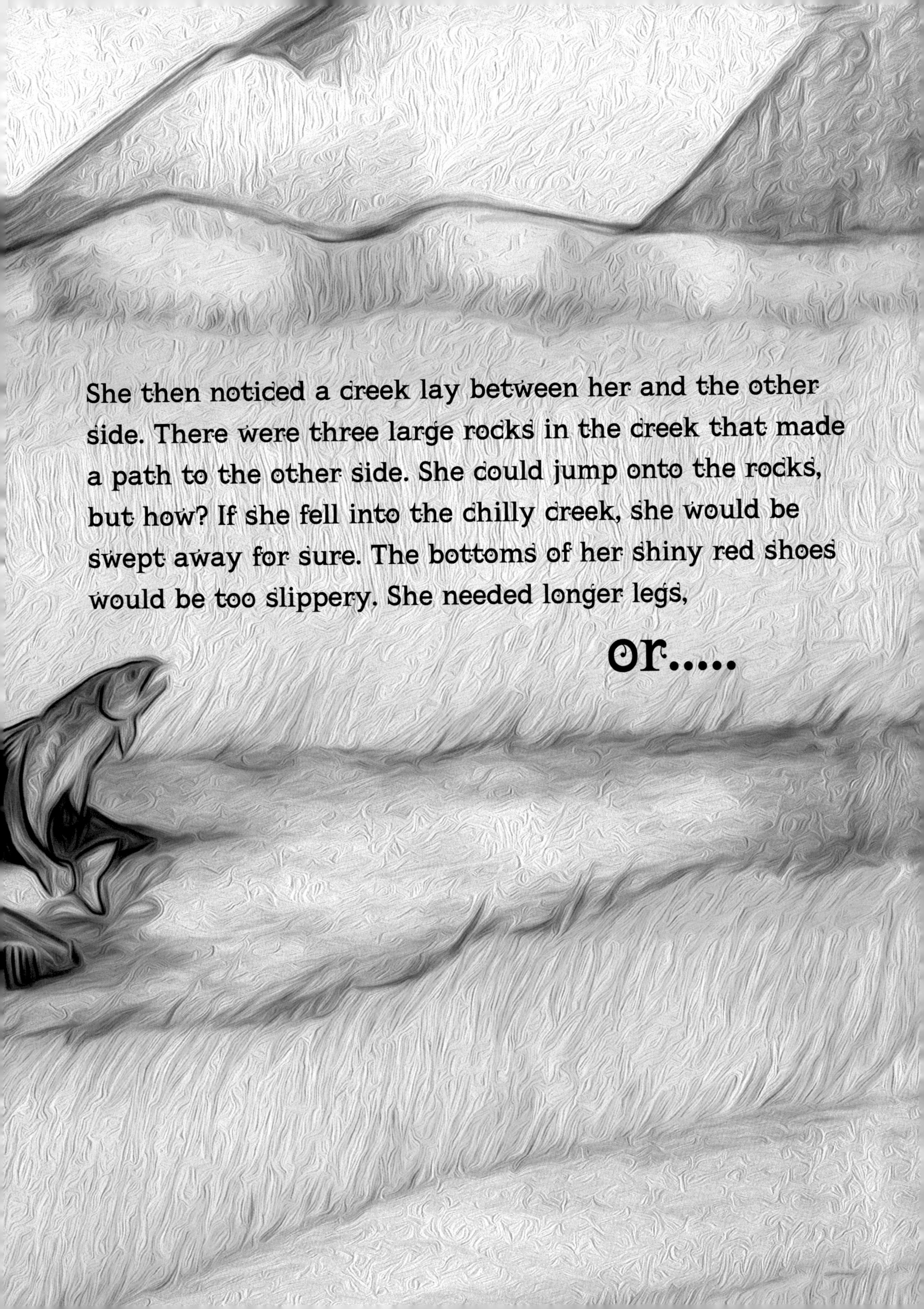

She then noticed a creek lay between her and the other side. There were three large rocks in the creek that made a path to the other side. She could jump onto the rocks, but how? If she fell into the chilly creek, she would be swept away for sure. The bottoms of her shiny red shoes would be too slippery. She needed longer legs,

or.....

“Daddy’s shoes!” Kimberlite said as she took them from her backpack.

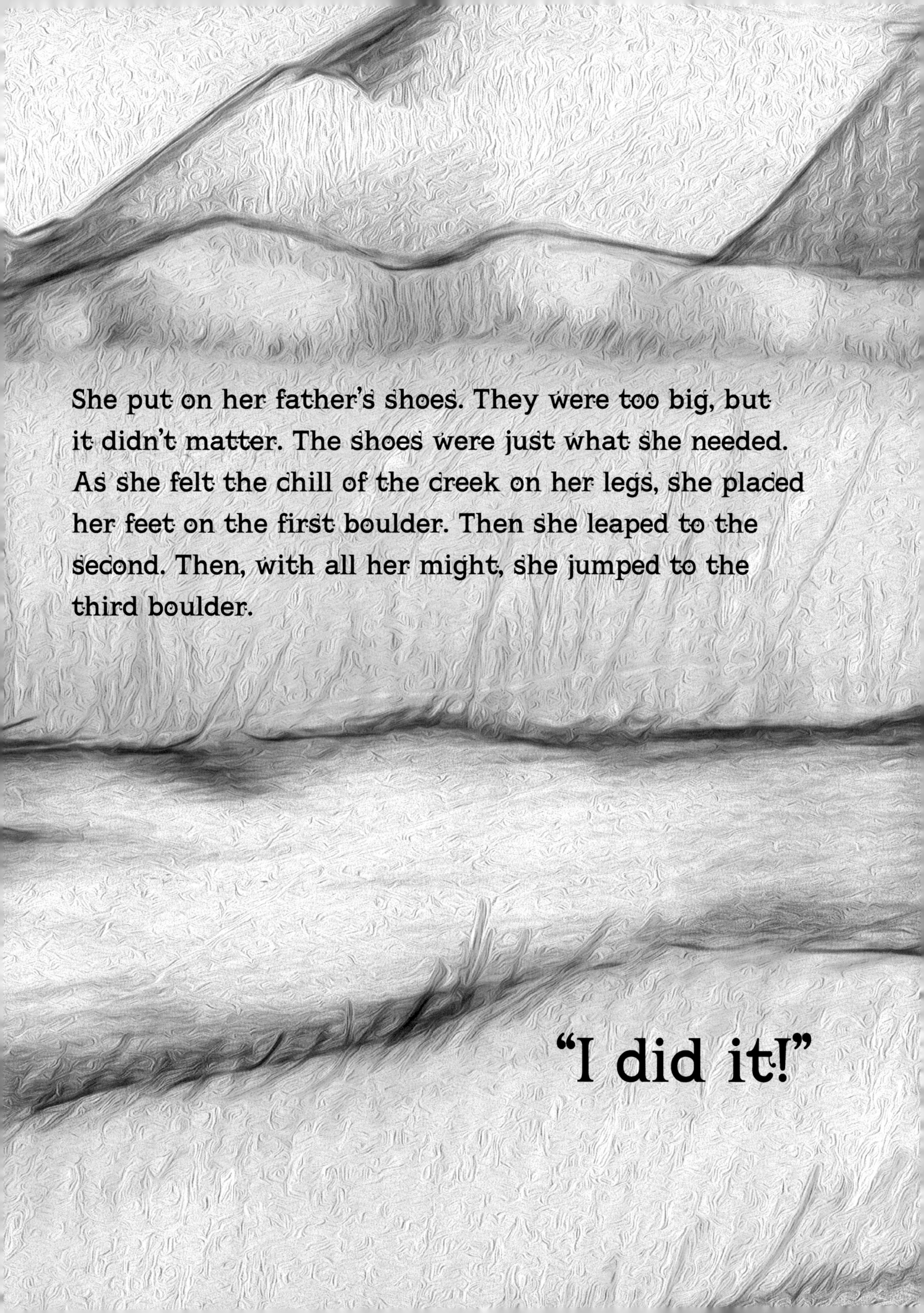

She put on her father's shoes. They were too big, but it didn't matter. The shoes were just what she needed. As she felt the chill of the creek on her legs, she placed her feet on the first boulder. Then she leaped to the second. Then, with all her might, she jumped to the third boulder.

"I did it!"

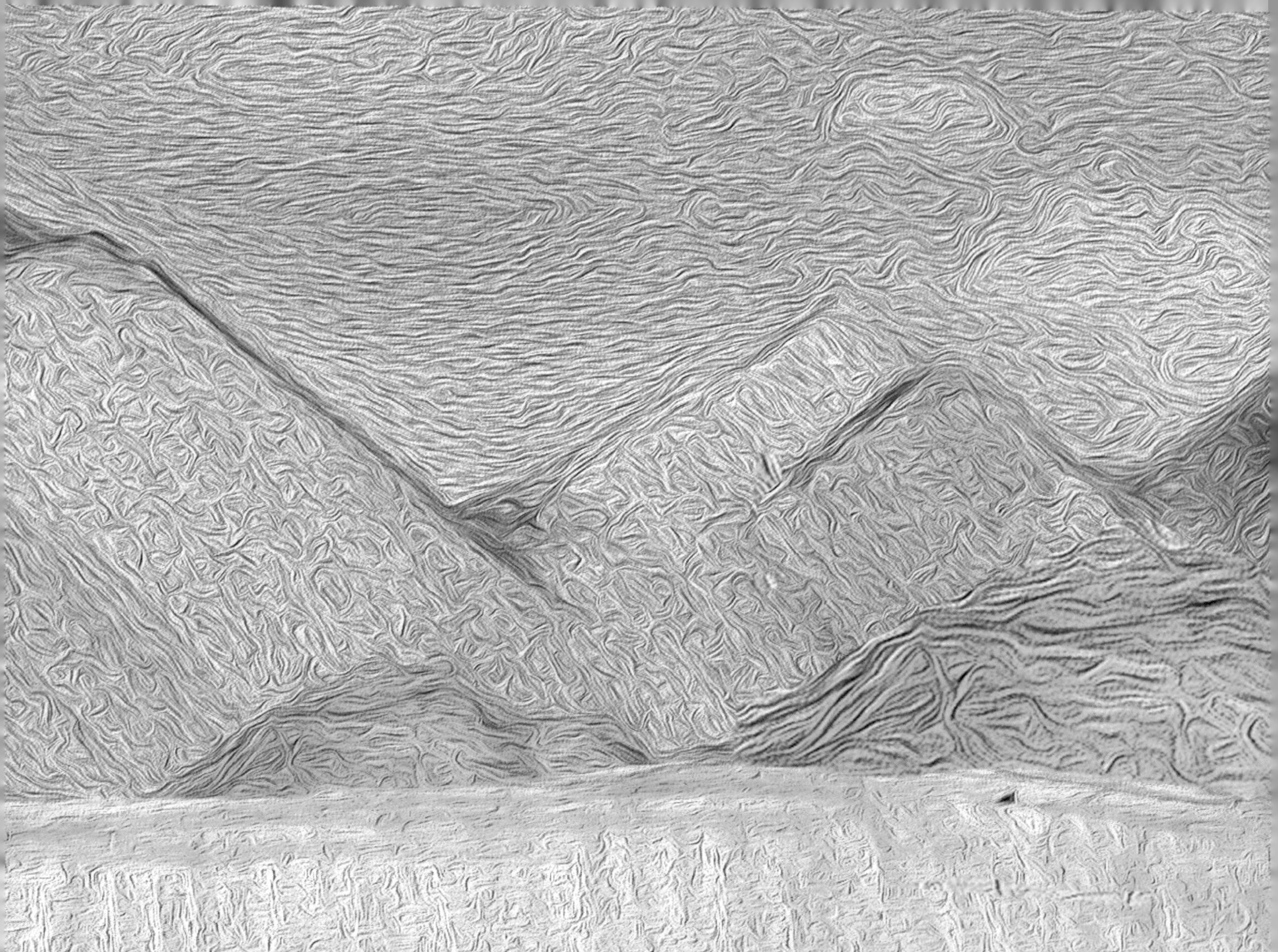

Kimberlite stood at the bottom of the mountain. She remembered her brothers saying, "If you reached the bottom of the mountain, you are close to finding the diamond."

She heard an echo in the wind that seemed to say, "You are not far away from it now. Stay on the right path."

Kimberlite listened, and continued her journey.

Just as Kimberlite began to skip in excitement, out jumped Rattlesnake. He startled her. He had been following her all along.

Again, he hissed that, the beautiful diamond that shines brighter than a lump of coal is not real.

"Be quiet!"

I WILL find the beautiful diamond that shines brighter than a lump of coal.

You'll see!" Kimberlite said as she placed her hands on her hips.

Just then, the tree near Kimberlite began to shake from the roar of a Black Bear. Both Kimberlite and Rattlesnake shook in fear.

"Little girl, don't listen to him!" roared Black Bear. "Rattlesnake is trying to keep you from finding the diamond."

Black Bear told Kimberlite that, the closer she got to the diamond, the more Rattlesnake was going to try to lead her in the wrong direction. He told her to run and not look back.

"Go!" Black Bear roared. "I will take care of Rattlesnake."

Now more than ever, Kimberlite wanted to find the diamond. She would not give up. Kimberlite ran!

Kimberlite finally, had come to the end of the trail. But, once again, she heard Rattlesnake saying, "You will not find the diamond that shines brighter than a lump of coal."

But this time, she didn't need Cougar to save her. She didn't need Black Bear. Rattlesnake began to hiss more, and more.

As Kimberlite continued on her way, she began to run. She had left the dark trail of the hollow, and saw a bright light.

“This must be it! It is! It is!” Kimberlite screamed in excitement.

She was now at the side of the mountain, at the end of the trail that her brothers and father had talked about. She took her nugget of coal, and began to dig. She dug, and she dug, and she dug.

All along, Rattlesnake watched and began hitting his head on the ground, “No, no, stop!” he hissed.

Kimberlite was too busy digging to care about Rattlesnake. Then, she stopped digging. She couldn’t believe her eyes.

She had uncovered a treasure chest! She opened it and found things she never imagined. There were pictures of people she knew. One was of her grandmother. Her grandmother still wore her hair in a bun at the top of her hair. And, she had on the pearl necklace and earrings she always wore on special occasions.

There was a picture of her father as a young man. He wore a brand new miner's hat, and his father, and grandfather posed with their miner's hats on too.

There was a picture of her father as a little boy. He held a nugget of coal just like the one he had given to her.

There was another picture of her grandfather in front of his church. He was a young, handsome man who became the church pastor.

As Kimberlite went farther into the chest, a light from within the chest began to shine brighter. Rattlesnake ran away as the light began to glow.

It was then that she discovered...

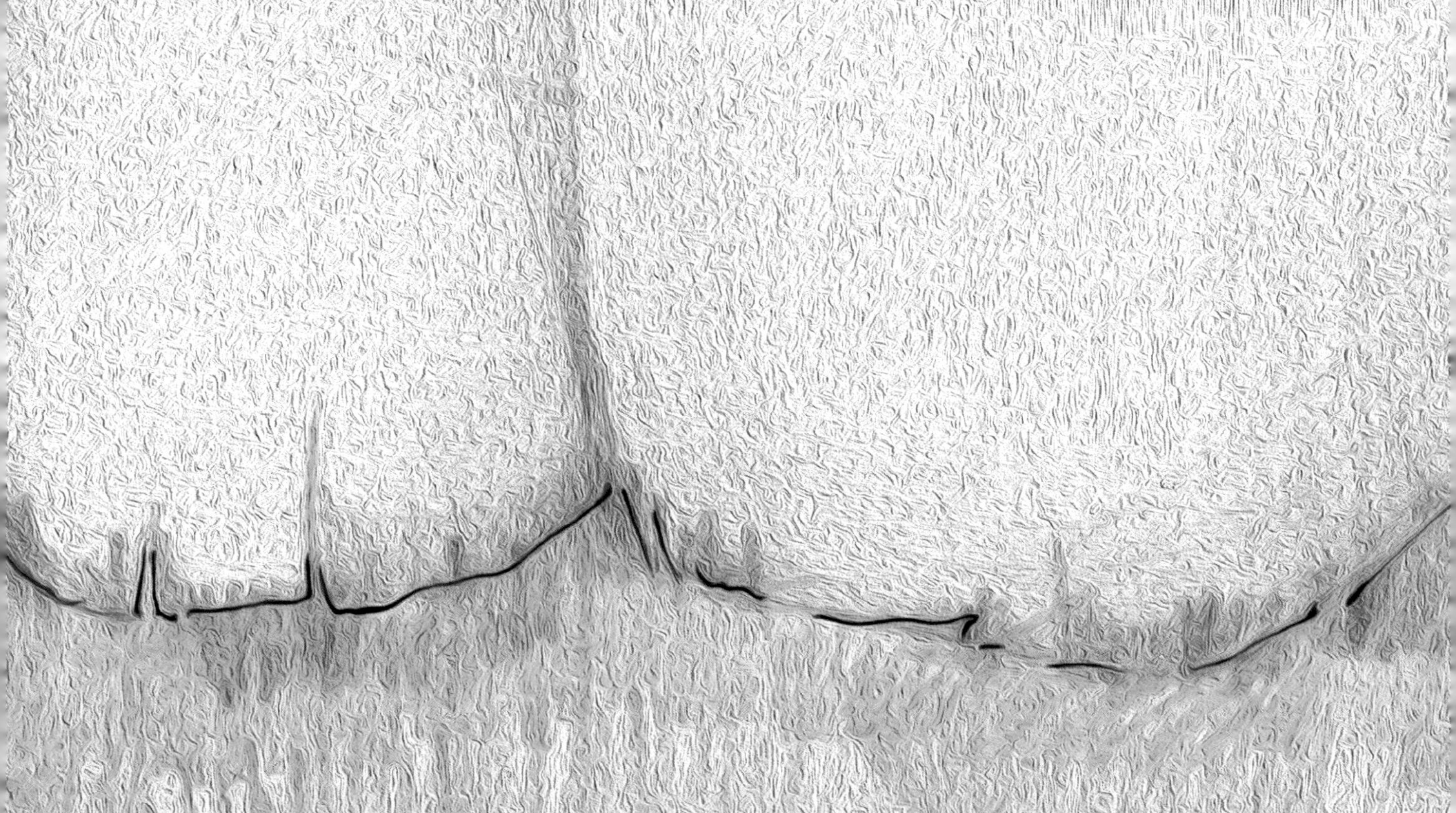

"A big beautiful diamond!" Kimberlite said as she jumped up and down. She placed it in her hand next to the large lump of coal.

"Here is the diamond that shines brighter than a lump of coal!"

She now knew that the diamond her father talked about was not one he needed to find, but one that had been lost years ago.

Kimberlite took off her father's shoes, and put on her own shiny red shoes. She placed the pictures in her backpack and left the heavy chest behind.

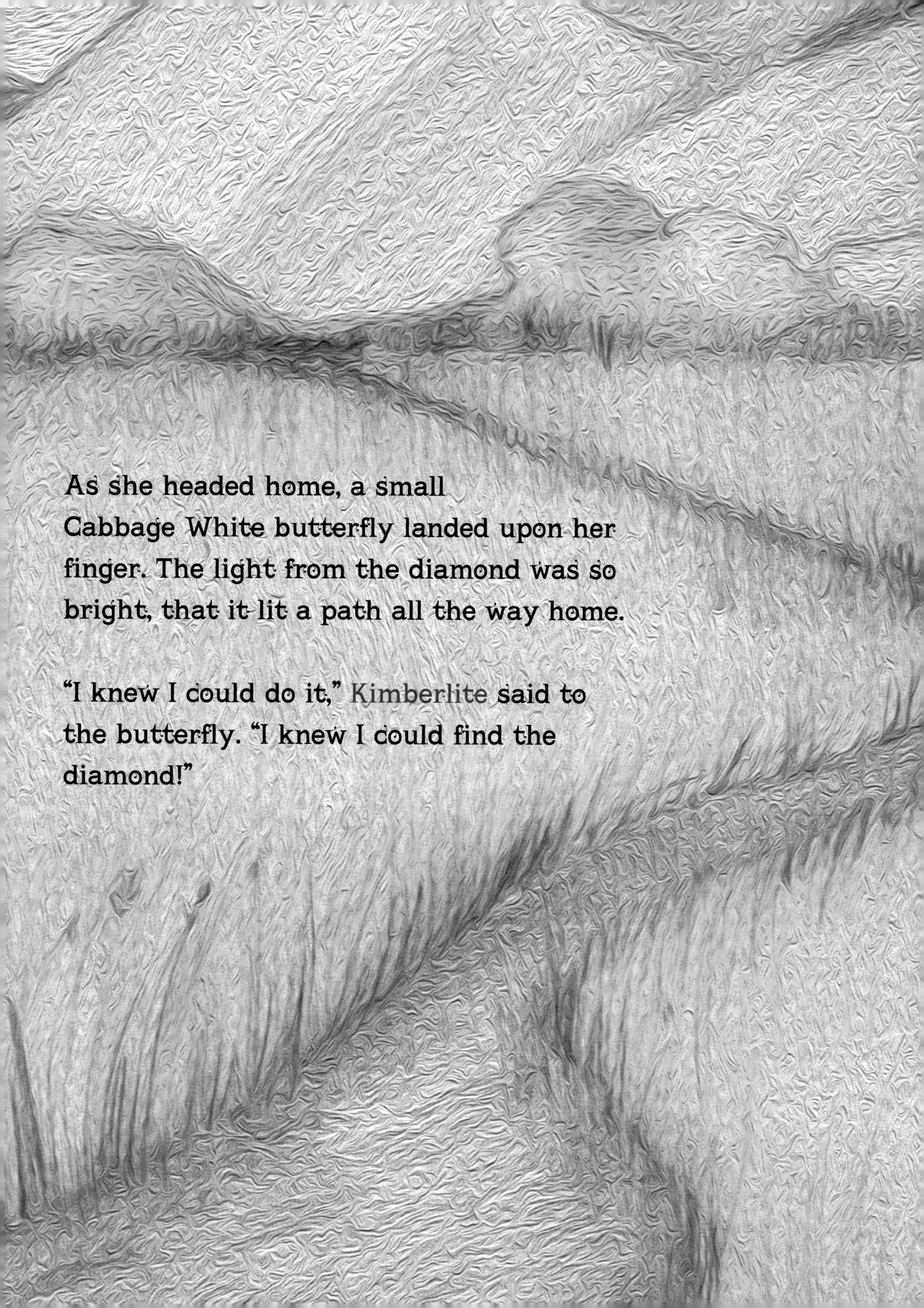

As she headed home, a small
Cabbage White butterfly landed upon her finger. The light from the diamond was so bright, that it lit a path all the way home.

"I knew I could do it," Kimberlite said to the butterfly. "I knew I could find the diamond!"

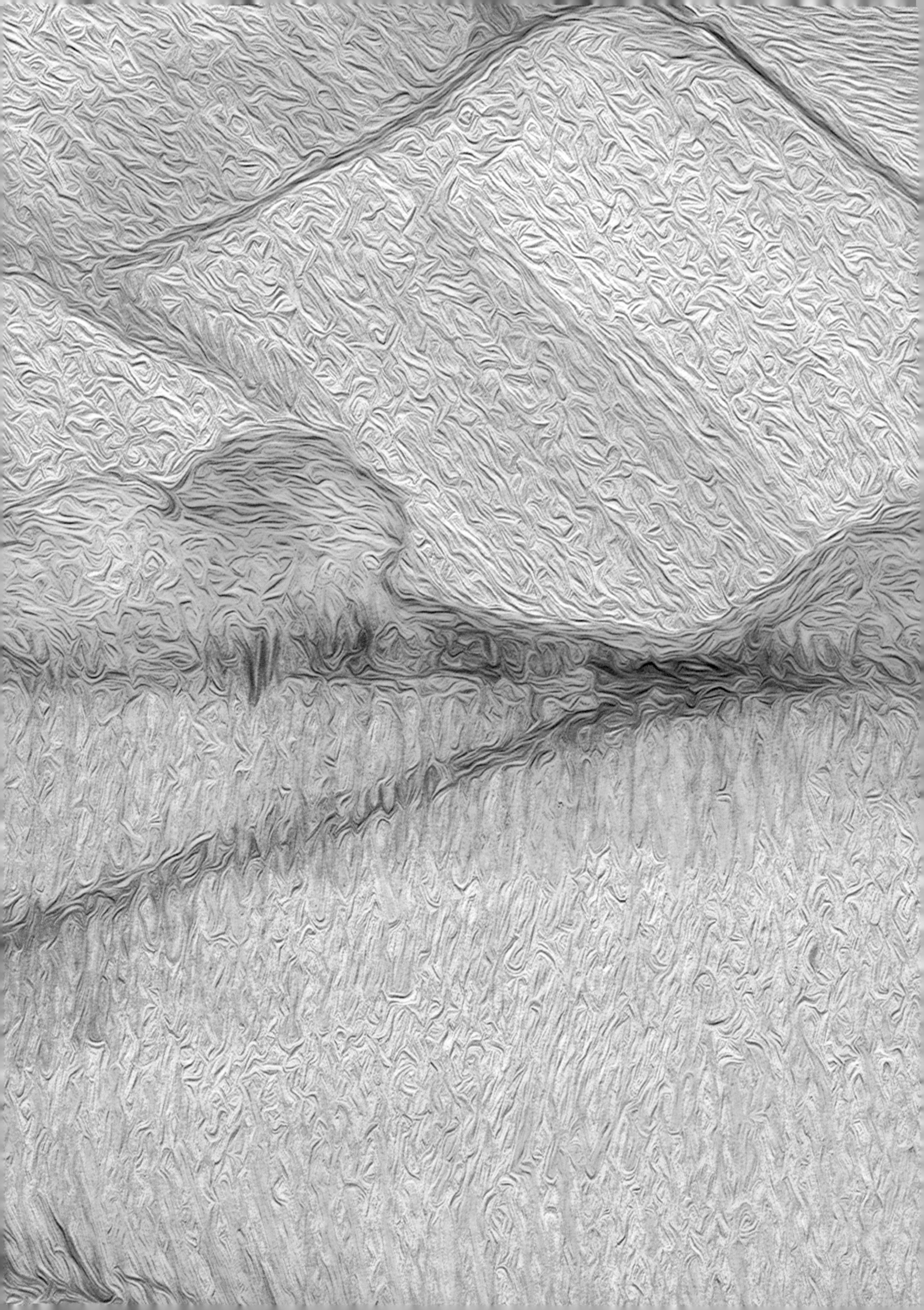

Kimberlite:

Kimberlite is an igneous rock best known for sometimes containing diamonds.

Hollow:

A small valley between the mountains

Questions for the Reader

Pre-read questions:

After looking at the cover, what do you think this story is about?

What are you curious to find out about Kimberlite?

During read questions:

When you found out the problem, what did you imagine would happen?

What is the setting of this story?

Who is the main character?

What conflict (problem) does the character have?

After read questions:

What was your favorite part of the story?

What would you add to the story?

What is something you would like to have an adventure to find? Why?

Published in collaboration with Season Press LLC & Fortitude Graphic Design and Printing.
Design and layout by Sean Hollins
Illustrated by Laurie H. Brady

In My Own Shoes: The Adventures of Kimberlite
may be purchased in bulk for educational, fund-raising, or sales promotional use. For more information, please e-mail charmaneechols@gmail.com

Echols, Charmane. *In My Own Shoes: The Adventures of Kimberlite*/ by Charmane Echols
p. cm Summary: In the hollows of West Virginia, Kimberlite's journey leads her to find the true diamond.

Library of Congress Control Number
2016955158

ISBN 978-0-9977136-2-6

Printed and published in the United States of America

First Edition
1 3 5 7 9 10 8 6 4 2

Made in the USA
Columbia, SC
18 April 2017